IMMA STATE

by
Jerry Tobias

This book is intended to introduce the states
to the Imma reader. It is not intended to present
an exacting study or complete picture of the many
and varied state functions and contributions. In
each poem, some state information is presented;
however, it by no means should suggest that this
covers the many wonderful things that each state
has to offer.

Imma hopes that the poems will stimulate an
interest in our states and encourage the reader to
further explore them.

Teddy Bear Press

Imma Says

Imma State
   for you to see;
here are some things
   that are found in me:

Cities

Politics

Size

Economy

Population

Flowers

Special Features
Special Events

Mountains

Government

industry

Education

Religions

People

Recreation

CROPS

Products

homes

Shape

Birds

Climate

Historical Events

ISBN 1-880017-16-4

Table of Contents

71. Imma Ohio
73. Imma Oklahoma
75. Imma Oregon
77. Imma Pennsylvania
79. Imma Rhode Island
81. Imma South Carolina
83. Imma South Dakota
85. Imma Tennessee
87. Imma Texas
89. Imma Utah
91. Imma Vermont
93. Imma Virginia
95. Imma Washington
97. Imma West Virginia
99. Imma Wisconsin
101. Imma Wyoming

Imma Says:
Here are the states
for you to see;
learn them well
and get an Imma State Degree

To Pank, Big Toby, Donna Marie,
and all my children,

Imma yours.

To Jamie for his desktop publishing and consultation, and to
Tina and Jackie for another look,

Imma yours, too.

To Oliver, Barney, Bozo, Max, and all my special friends,

Imma especially yours.

**Michigan –
Home State of
IMMA**

Imma books
    will help you learn;
they deal with subjects
    of concern.

The verse is meaningful
    and lots of fun;
it can be understood
    by everyone.

The Imma pictures
    will educate;
they make it easy
    to communicate.

So read your Imma
    and learn from it;
you'll find the teachings
    a benefit.

Introduction

Imma state
    for you to see;
I'd like to share
    all about me.

I was born into statehood
    like all others;
I have a birthdate
    like your sisters and brothers.

I have cities
    for you to know;
I think it's important
    as they will help you grow.

I feel you should know
    what I've done;
I think my background
    is kind of fun.

I think it's important
    that you know what I do;
I feel that this will help you
    grow, too.

I want you to know
    about each state;
I feel you will learn
    from what Imma will relate.

Imma state
    with this final say,
"Read about me
    and enlighten your day."

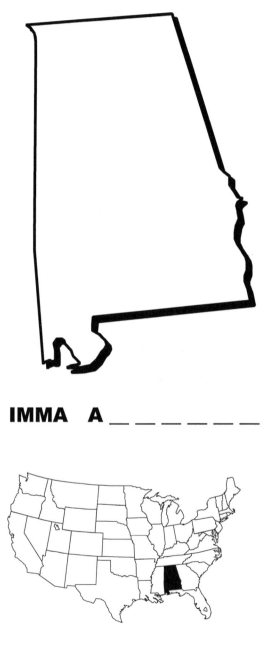

IMMA   A _ _ _ _ _ _ _

Imma Alabama

Imma Alabama
    or southern state;
I have a 1819
    birthdate.

I'm shaped like a stapler
    in a funny sort of way;
I think that you will have
    to let your imagination play.

I have mountains and rivers
    for you to see;
I have rich farmlands and forests
    that characterize me.

I have Mobile and Montgomery
    with a city name;
I have Birmingham
    with an Alabama claim.

I grow cotton
    and produce lumber;
I also provide produce
    in great number.

I have a nice climate
    with resorts to stay;
I provide nice surroundings
    to vacation away.

Imma Alabama
    with this for you,
"I have many sights
    for you to view."

IMMA   A _ _ _ _ _

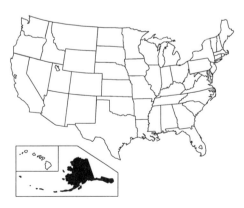

Imma Alaska

Imma Alaska
    or northwestern state;
I have a 1959
    birthdate.

I'm shaped like a head
    with a ponytail;
I think your imagination will help
    with my shaping detail.

I have mountains and rivers
    and forests to see;
I have many natural features
    that characterize me.

I have Juneau, Fairbanks,
    and Anchorage with a city name;
I have Nome and Sitka
    with an Alaskan claim.

I abound with fish
    and timber, too;
I also produce minerals
    and oil for you.

I'm a very big state
    that's hard to get around;
I need a snowmobile or dogsled
    to cover my ground.

Imma Alaska
    with this tidbit,
"I paid Russia millions
    for my purchase permit."

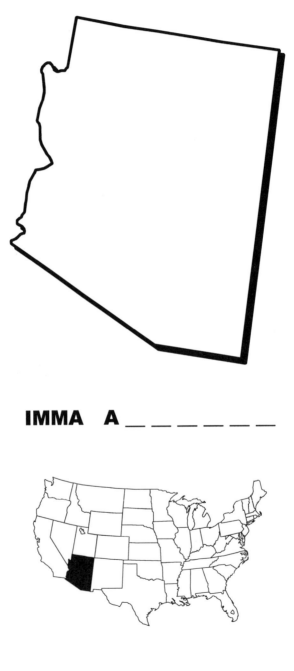

IMMA   A _ _ _ _ _ _ _

Imma Arizona

Imma Arizona
      or southwestern state;
I have a 1912
      birthdate.

I'm shaped like a puzzle
      or part of one;
this is the best I can do
      for shaping fun.

I have Mesa, Tempe,
      and Phoenix with a city name;
I have Tucson and Glendale
      with an Arizona claim.

I provide sun and warmth
      and much to do;
I offer retirement
      and a healthful life for you.

I offer walking and skiing
      and exercise for you;
I have golf and tennis
      and biking, too.

I find that tourism
      is big in my state;
it increases my growth
      and population rate.

Imma Arizona
      with this to relate,
"God has blessed
      my healthful state."

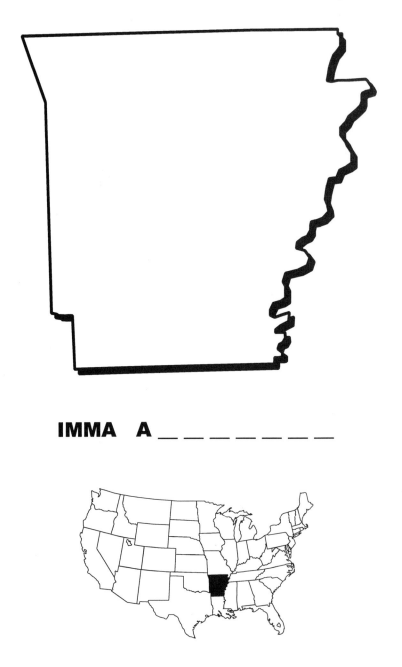

IMMA A _ _ _ _ _ _ _ _

Imma Arkansas

Imma Arkansas
    or south central state;
I have a 1836
    birthdate.

I look like a headlight
    on an old-fashioned car;
I guess my imagination
    may have gone too far.

I have mountains, highlands,
    and rivers, too;
I have forests, prairies, and
    lowlands to view.

I supply many products
    with an Arkansas say;
I'm big on cotton
    and lumber today.

I also produce apples, grapes,
    and tomatoes;
I produce peanuts, peaches,
    and potatoes.

I have created Hot Springs,
    a healthy place to go;
I find it relaxing
    to sit and let my mineral water flow.

Imma Arkansas
    that would infer,
"I think you would enjoy
    being an Arkansas traveler."

IMMA   C _ _ _ _ _ _ _ _ _

Imma California

Imma California
        or western state;
I have an 1850
        birthdate.

I've a leg-like shape
        that borders the sea;
I have the Pacific Ocean
        that's next to me.

I have beautiful cities
        and towns to see;
I have many communities
        for you and me.

I have mountains and cliffs
        for you to view;
I have beaches, forests,
        and deserts, too.

I've a climate
        with quite a range;
I'm usually warm
        but I'm subject to change.

I have Hollywood
        where movies come to be;
I have San Francisco,
        with many sights to see.

Imma California
        with this say,
"Come and visit
        and you might stay."

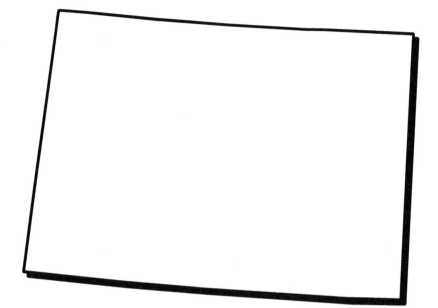

IMMA C _ _ _ _ _ _ _ _

Imma Colorado

Imma Colorado
    or western state;
I have an 1876
    birthdate.

I'm rectangular or square-like
    in shape;
I have a most interesting
    squarescape.

I have big mountains
    on which to ski;
I also have trails and runs
    for the ski bunny.

I'm a fresh-air state
    with a healthy view;
I provide stress relief
    and relaxation, too.

I have Denver and Colorado Springs
    with much to see;
I provide many sights
    for you and me.

I promote skiing
    and winter sports;
I have many
    winter resorts.

Imma Colorado
    with this decree,
"You must come to Colorado
    and ski with me."

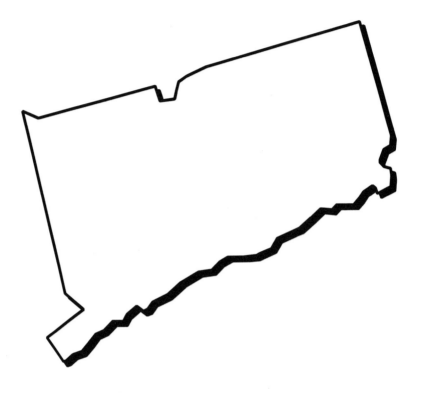

IMMA C _ _ _ _ _ _ _ _ _ _ _

Imma Connecticut

Imma Connecticut
    or northeastern state;
I have an 1788
    birthdate.

I'm a small state
    with an upside down cannon-like shape;
you must use your imagination
    to visualize my cannonscape.

I have bear mountain
    and lovely scenery to see;
I have a southern border
    that gets me to the sea.

I have Bridgeport, Waterbury,
    and Stamford with a city claim;
I have New Haven and Hartford
    with a Connecticut claim.

I'm very productive
    and produce a lot;
I make needles and pins
    and other products I've got.

I was first
    with a constitution to write;
it was acceptable
    and done just right.

Imma Connecticut
    with this final say,
"When you think of traveling,
    think of Connecticut today."

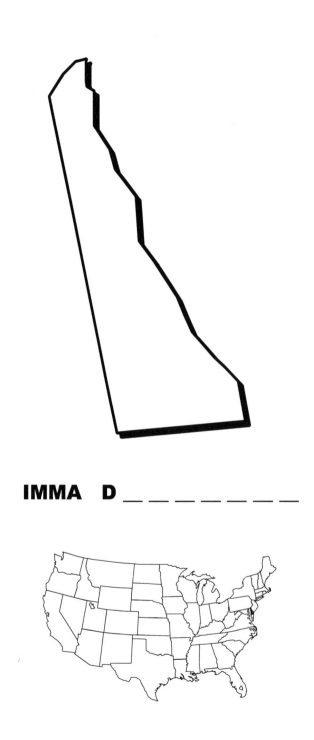

IMMA D _ _ _ _ _ _ _

Imma Delaware

Imma Delaware
     or middle Atlantic state;
I have an 1787
     birthdate.

I'm long and narrow
     with a sled-like shape;
I could also be a skate
     on your imagination-scape.

I have Dover and Newark
     as cities to see;
I have Wilmington and Brookside
     that Delaware me.

I have nice areas
     with sights to see;
I have Delaware Bay,
     which is next to me.

I use my Bay
     to boat and fish;
I can provide
     a tasty fish dish.

I also farm
     and produce fruit;
I grow an apple
     that's a Delaware beaut.

Imma Delaware
     with this say,
"Come and fish
     in my Delaware Bay."

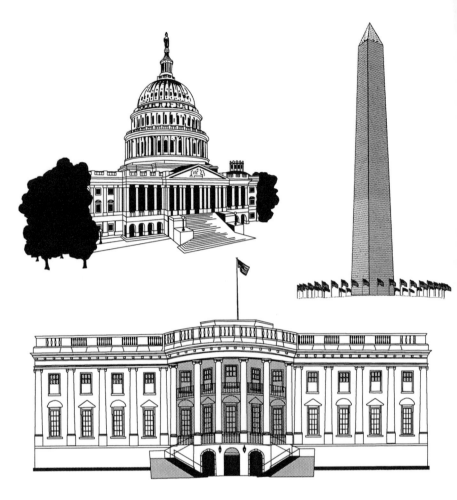

IMMA D _ _ _ _ _ _ _
of C _ _ _ _ _ _ _

Imma District of Columbia

Imma District of Columbia
　　and I'm not a state;
I'm really without
　　a state birthdate.

I was selected by Congress
　　for this role;
I was to represent our country
　　and its goal.

I have great buildings, museums,
　　and monuments for you;
I have many sights
　　for the visitor to view.

I house the government
　　and leaders, too;
I house many agencies
　　that represent you.

I have congressional people
　　and judges who preside;
I have many leaders
　　who make decisions and decide.

I house the President
　　in the White House;
I house him there
　　with his daughter and spouse.

Imma District of Columbia
　　with this decree,
"I wish you'd take time
　　and visit with me."

IMMA F _ _ _ _ _ _ _

Imma Florida

Imma Florida
    or southeastern state;
I have an 1845
    birthdate.

I'm shaped like a drill holder
    in an imaginative way;
I have sunshine and beaches
    with a recreational say.

I'm surrounded by water
    as you can see;
I also have lakes, swamps,
    and rivers all over me.

I have beautiful cities
    for you to view;
I have Miami, Orlando,
    and Tampa for you.

I'm a big producer
    of citrus fruit;
I dress my oranges
    in a round orange suit.

I provide places to see
    and things to do;
I have many attractions
    that will excite you.

Imma Florida
    with this say,
"I'm a leading state
    to visit and play."

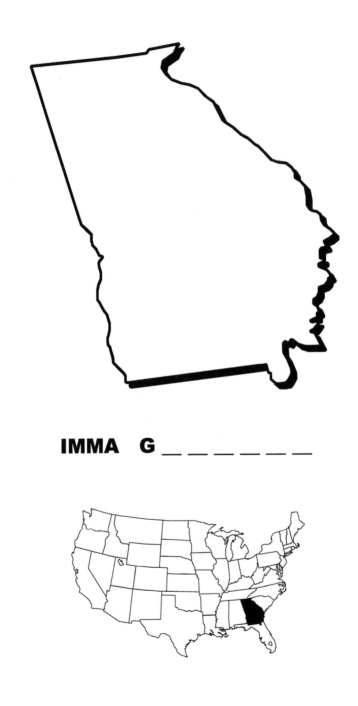

IMMA   G _ _ _ _ _ _ _

Imma Georgia

Imma Georgia
    or southern state;
I have a 1788
    birthdate.

I'm shaped like a sled
    if you look at me right;
I think imagination helps
    to keep my sled in sight.

I have several cities
    with a Georgia claim;
I have Atlanta, Savannah,
    and Columbus with a city name.

I have mountains, rivers,
    and winding streams;
I have forests and waterfalls
    that provide scenic dreams.

I grow cotton
    and other crops;
I produce pecans and peanuts,
    which fill my shops.

I also produce eggs and peaches
    in my state;
I ship them all over
    to fill your plate.

Imma Georgia
    with this decree,
"When you eat peaches,
    please think of me."

IMMA H _ _ _ _ _

Imma Hawaii

Imma Hawaii
    or far western state;
I have a 1959
    birthdate.

I'm an island state
    with an island chain;
I'm shaped like puzzle pieces
    with unusual terrain.

I have mountains, beaches,
    and flowers to see;
I have volcanoes, plants,
    and many a tree.

I have beautiful cities
    that characterize me;
I have Honolulu and Hilo
    for you to see.

I house people
    from many backgrounds;
I have a mix
    that occupies my grounds.

I'm surrounded by water
    and offer a lot of recreation;
I provide surfing, sunning, and swimming
    for your vacation.

Imma Hawaii,
    your pleasure envoy,
"Take a trip
    and come and enjoy."

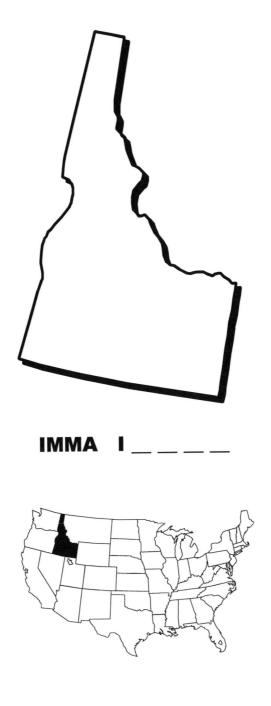

IMMA I _ _ _ _

Imma Idaho

Imma Idaho
    or northwestern state;
I have a 1890
    birthdate.

I'm shaped like a stamp maker
    when you visualize me;
it takes some imagination
    for a stamp maker to see.

I have Pocatello, Lewiston,
    and Nampa with a city name;
I have Idaho Falls and Boise
    with an Idaho claim.

I'm known for potatoes
    the world around;
I raise Idahos
    in my ground.

I like my Idahos
    and the way they taste;
I eat the skins
    so there's no waste.

I send my Idahos
    all over the states;
I find my Idahos
    on many plates.

Imma Idaho
    with this say,
"I supply my Idahos
    to the U.S. today."

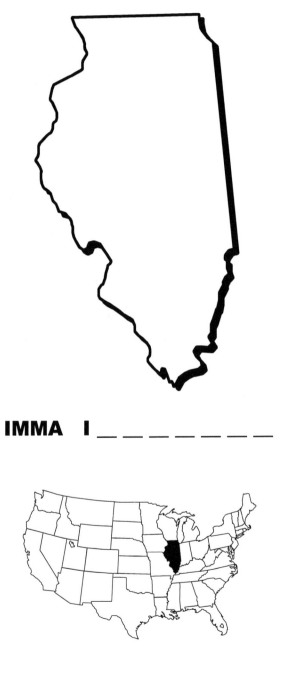

IMMA I _ _ _ _ _ _ _ _

Imma Illinois

Imma Illinois
    or north central state;
I have an 1818
    birthdate.

I'm shaped like an animal
    on the run;
you must use your imagination
    and have some fun.

I have sizable cities
    like Chicago and Aurora;
I also have Springfield
    and Peoria.

I guess when you think of me,
    you think of Chicago by call;
I find that Chicago
    seems to have it all.

I find big buildings
    and shopping galore;
I find popular eating places
    and every kind of store.

I find transportation
    at its very best;
I find planes and trains
    never, never rest.

Imma Illinois
    with this smile,
"Come to Chicago
    and stay awhile."

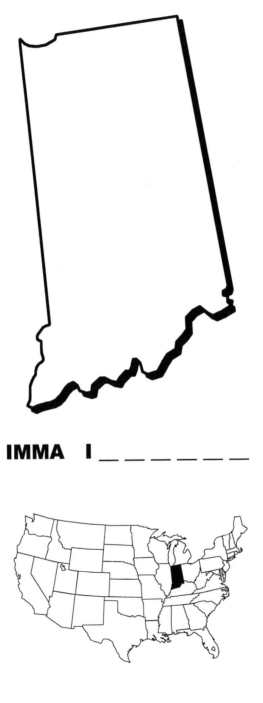

IMMA I _ _ _ _ _ _ _

Imma Indiana

Imma Indiana
    or north central state;
I have an 1816
    birthdate.

I'm a boot-shaped state
    with rolling land;
I have lakes and rivers
    and dunes of sand.

I have Evansville and Gary
    with a city claim;
I have Fort Wayne, South Bend,
    and Indianapolis with a city name.

I grow corn, soybeans,
    and wheat;
I find my crops
    are hard to beat.

I also manufacture products
    for the world to see;
I make several items
    that characterize me.

I have a speedway
    where cars race;
I like the excitement,
    competition, and fast pace.

Imma Indiana
    with this say,
"You should come to Indiana
    and see my speedway."

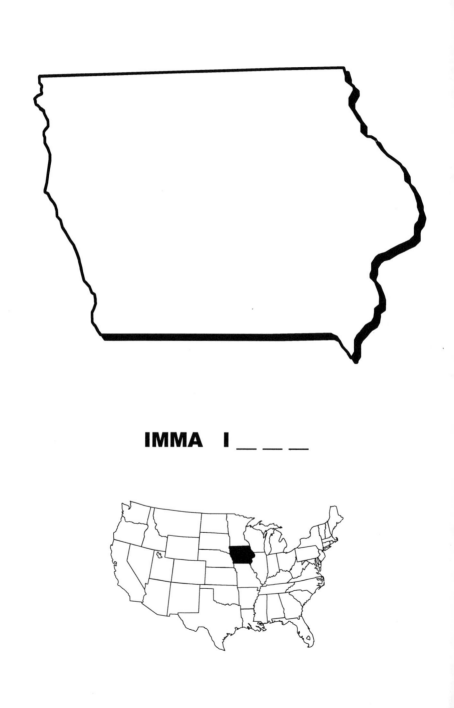

IMMA I _ _ _

Imma Iowa

Imma Iowa
     or north central state;
I have an 1846
     birthdate.

I'm a square state
     with fertile land;
I'm virtually
     a farmer's wonderland.

I have Davenport and Waterloo
     with a city claim;
I have Sioux City, Des Moines,
     and Cedar Rapids with a city name.

I'm a farming state
     with many farmhands;
I've a big chunk
     of America's farmlands.

I produce corn, soybeans,
     and barley, too;
I also raise
     livestock for you.

I manufacture goods
     in my state;
I make fertilizers and chemicals
     that improve my farm production rate.

Imma Iowa
     with this say,
"If you want to farm,
     come down Iowa way."

IMMA K _ _ _ _ _ _

Imma Kansas

Imma Kansas
    or central state;
I have an 1861
    birthdate.

I'm rectangular or square-like
    in shape;
I have a rich soil
    and a fine farmscape.

I'm basically
    a farm state;
I produce products
    for your plate.

I grow wheat
    and corn, too;
I produce oats, beans,
    and barley for you.

I have cities
    that support my farm claim;
I have Topeka, Kansas City,
    and Wichita by name.

I sell my products
    in every grocery shop;
I'm very proud
    of my Kansas crop.

Imma Kansas
    with this say,
"I farm for you
    every day."

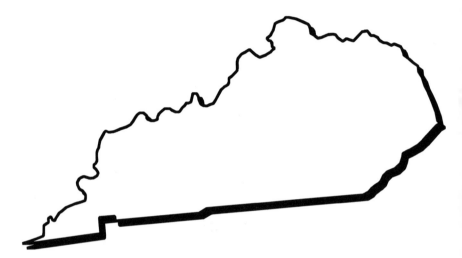

IMMA K _ _ _ _ _ _ _ _

Imma Kentucky

Imma Kentucky
> or east central state;
I have a 1792
> birthdate.

I'm shaped like a sled
> with Santa inside;
I hope you can imagine
> my sled-shaped ride.

I have mountains and hills
> and level ground;
I have forests and rivers
> and bluegrass by the pound.

I have cities
> like Frankfort and Covington;
I also have Louisville
> and Lexington.

I love to raise horses
> that are something to see;
they are big and beautiful
> and represent me.

I have the Kentucky Derby
> where horses race;
I love the activity
> and fast pace.

Imma Kentucky
> with this about me,
"Don't miss the Derby,
> it's something to see."

IMMA L _ _ _ _ _ _ _ _ _

Imma Louisiana

Imma Louisiana
    or southern state;
I have an 1812
    birthdate.

I'm shaped like a boot
    with many waterways;
I have marshlands, rivers,
    and lots of bays.

I have New Orleans and Shreveport
    with a city name;
I have Lafayette and Baton Rouge
    with a Louisiana claim.

I have lots of old places
    to enjoy and see;
I also have the new
    for you and me.

I find timber big
    and fishing, too;
I also produce soybeans
    and sugarcane for you.

I host the Mardi Gras
    and a lot of jazz;
I love the celebration
    and the razzmatazz.

Imma Louisiana
    with this law,
"You must come to New Orleans
    for my Mardi Gras."

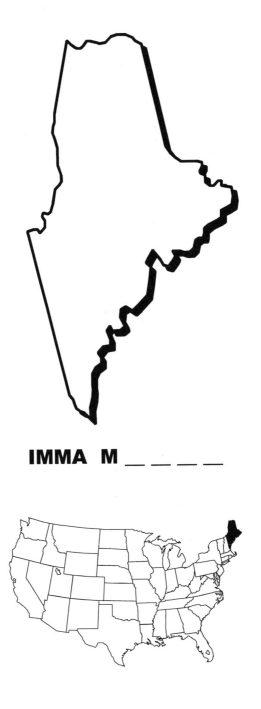

IMMA M _ _ _ _

Imma Maine

Imma Maine
    or northeastern state;
I have an 1820
    birthdate.

I'm shaped like an animal head
    in a shapely way;
you must be imaginative
    to see this display.

I have a picturesque seacoast
    with harbors to see;
I have lakes and lighthouses
    that portray me.

I have cities and villages
    that add to my looks;
I find them charming
    with their buildings and brooks.

I provide farmlands
    and fishing grounds, too;
I can provide fish and potatoes
    for you.

I'm a good place
    for recreation and rest;
I'm always ready
    for you and a guest.

Imma Maine
    with this say,
"Please visit my state
    and you will enjoy your stay."

IMMA M _ _ _ _ _ _ _ _

Imma Maryland

Imma Maryland
　　or middle Atlantic state;
I have a 1788
　　birthdate.

I'm shaped like a spray nozzle
　　as you can see;
I have rivers and streams
　　that empty into the sea.

I'm divided in two
　　by the Chesapeake Bay;
I consider the Chesapeake
　　my water throughway.

I find it navigable
　　and easy to use;
I can move products
　　by boat as I choose.

I catch crabs
　　from the Chesapeake Bay;
I gather each catch
　　and boat them away.

I have cities and towns
　　that support what I do;
I have them process my catch
　　and ship it to you.

Imma Maryland
　　with this "crabby" say,
"Please eat my crabs
　　from the Chesapeake Bay."

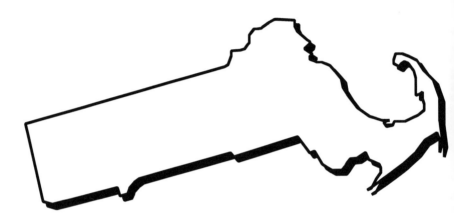

IMMA M _ _ _ _ _ _ _ _ _ _ _ _ — —

Imma Massachusetts

Imma Massachusetts
    or northeastern state;
I have a 1788
    birthdate.

I'm shaped like a bottle opener
    as you can see;
it doesn't take much
    to see a bottle opener in me.

I've got old communities
    and towns to view;
I've got old buildings
    and churches, too.

I've big cities
    with a history book claim;
I've Boston and Plymouth
    of historical fame.

I've got a history
    of early schools for you;
I helped to establish
    a model government, too.

I've a history
    of an early election try;
I also started town meetings
    to question the who, what, and why.

Imma Massachusetts
    with this final claim,
"I'm best known
    for my historical fame."

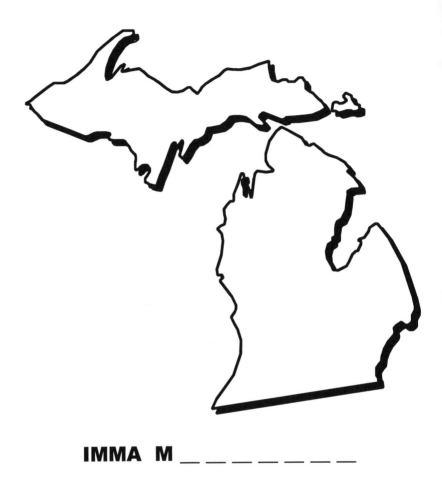

IMMA M _ _ _ _ _ _ _ _

Imma Michigan

Imma Michigan
     or north central state;
I have an 1837
     birthdate.

I have an upper and lower peninsula
     that divides me in two;
I have a bridge
     that's a connecting avenue.

I'm shaped like a mitten
     with a shark overhead;
I hope you will picture
     what you just read.

I have interesting cities and towns
     for you to view;
I have Detroit, Charlevoix,
     and Mackinac Island, too.

I'm both an industrial
     and agricultural state;
I'm a big producer
     with a highly productive rate.

I'm very big
     in making cars for you;
I find car making
     the biggest thing I do.

Imma Michigan
     with this say,
"Come to Michigan
     and buy a car today."

IMMA M _ _ _ _ _ _ _ _ _

Imma Minnesota

Imma Minnesota
      or north central state;
I have an 1858
      birthdate.

I'm shaped like a church
      if you look at me right;
I find my shape
      a church-like sight.

I'm full of lakes
      for you to see;
I have streams and waterfalls
      that characterize me.

I have Minneapolis and St. Paul
      with a city name;
I have Duluth and Rochester
      with a Minnesota claim.

I have nice homes
      with tree-filled yards and street;
I have quiet neighborhoods
      that are comfortable and complete.

I have places that entertain
      and cultural centers to see;
I have malls for shopping
      and recreation for you and me.

Imma Minnesota
      with this narrative,
"I think that you will find Minnesota
      a nice place to live."

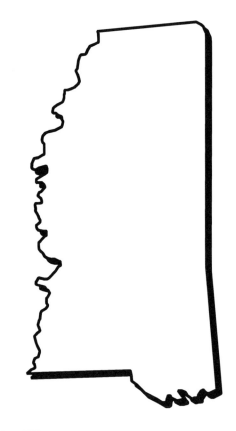

IMMA M _ _ _ _ _ _ _ _ _ _ _ _ _

Imma Mississippi

Imma Mississippi
    or southern state;
I have a 1817
    birthdate.

I'm shaped like a cracker
    with a bite out of it;
you'll need your imagination
    to see my biting bit.

I'm a flat-landed state
    with hills to see;
I have forests and woods
    that cover me.

I have Biloxi and Jackson
    with a city claim;
I have Vicksburg and Meridian
    with a city name.

I have historical mansions
    and old buildings to view;
I have modern construction
    that's ongoing, too.

I have a rural Mississippi
    and an urban one as well;
I have a mix
    where people dwell.

Imma Mississippi
    with this decree,
"I think that everyone should know
    how to spell Mi__ __i__ __i__ __i."

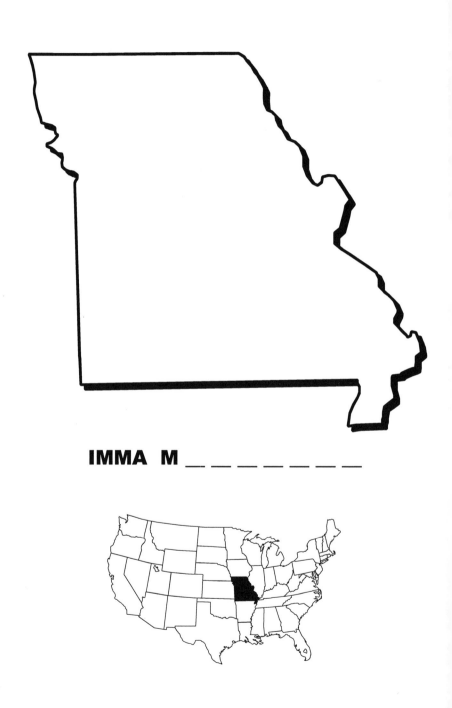

IMMA M _ _ _ _ _ _ _ _

Imma Missouri

Imma Missouri
    or central state;
I have an 1821
    birthdate.

I'm shaped like a face
    when you turn me around;
you must use your imagination
    until I'm found.

I have hills and fertile plains
    and rivers to see;
I have woods and open land
    that characterize me.

I have St. Louis and Kansas City
    with a city name;
I have Springfield, Saint Joseph, and Independence
    with a Missouri claim.

I have urban residential areas
    with shops and malls, too;
I have farming communities
    with rural living for you.

I farm soybeans and corn
    for you to eat;
I produce Missouri food products
    that are a treat.

Imma Missouri
    with this to say,
"I also have health resorts
    that will relax your cares away."

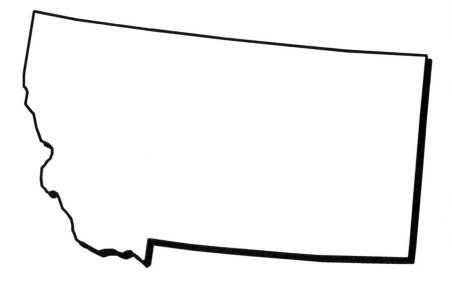

IMMA M _ _ _ _ _ _ _

Imma Montana

Imma Montana
 or northwestern state;
I have an 1889
 birthdate.

I'm shaped like an animal
 lying on the ground;
you must use your imagination
 and turn me around.

I have mountains and plains
 that cover me;
I'm a sight
 that you must see.

I have cities that are modern
 and offer much,
yet they still provide
 an Old West touch.

I have old battlefields and
 mining camps to view;
I have Indian reservations
 that characterize me, too.

I use names of places
 from the past;
their meaning and memory
 will always last.

Imma Montana
 with this say,
"The Old West
 lives on with me today."

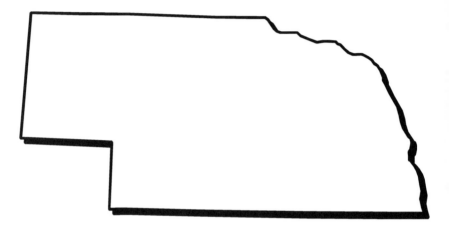

IMMA N _ _ _ _ _ _ _

Imma Nebraska

Imma Nebraska
    or central state;
I have an 1867
    birthdate.

I'm shaped like a cannon
    in an imaginative sense;
I look like a cannon
    with some pretense.

I have hills, rolling prairies,
    and grass-covered grounds;
I have rivers and canyons
    and sandy mounds.

I have Omaha and Lincoln
    with a city name;
I have Grand Island and North Platte
    with a Nebraska claim.

I provide city living
    and country life for you;
I find each provides a nice place
    to live and do.

I provide schools and churches
    and services for you;
I have stores and restaurants
    and recreation, too.

Imma Nebraska
    with this give,
"I find Nebraska
    a nice place to live."

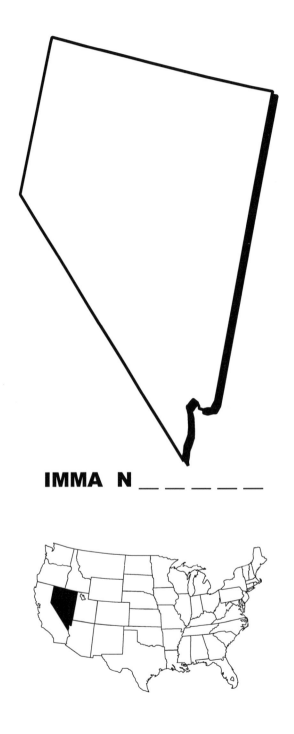

IMMA N _ _ _ _ _ _

Imma Nevada

Imma Nevada
    or western state;
I have an 1864
    birthdate.

I'm shaped like a chimney
    sitting on a rooftop;
I can be seen
    on a home or shop.

I have deserts, plains,
    and mountains to view;
I have dams and lakes
    to see, too.

I have Las Vegas and Reno
    where visitors come to play;
I'm an entertainment center
    for the U.S.A.

I have lavish hotels
    with swimming pools;
I have sun decks
    and whirlpools.

I provide gambling
    and big-time shows;
I have popular entertainers
    and well-known impresarios.

Imma Nevada
    with this say,
"Come to Nevada
    and vacation and play."

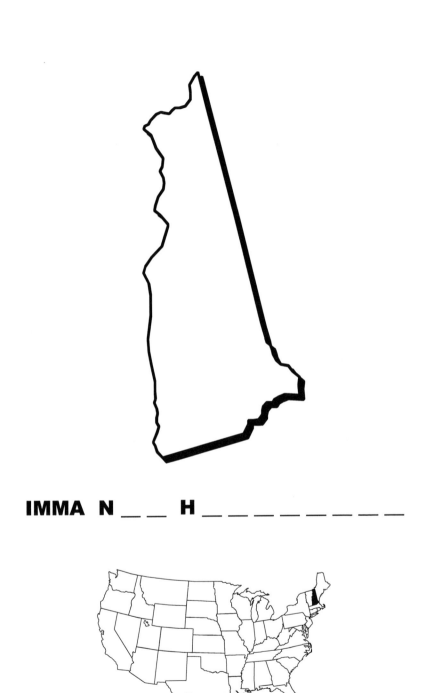

IMMA N _ _ H _ _ _ _ _ _ _ _ _

Imma New Hampshire

Imma New Hampshire
    or northeastern state;
I have a 1788
    birthdate.

I'm shaped like a key
    when you visualize me;
you must use your imagination
    to see my key.

I have Manchester, Derry, and Concord
    with a city name;
I have Nashua and Rochester
    with a New Hampshire claim.

I have mountains, lakes,
    and lowlands, too;
I have a lot of sights
    for you to view.

I've residential areas
    with schools and places to worship;
I've mall facilities
    with a store-laden shopping strip.

I have recreation programs
    with climbing, trailing, and hiking;
I also have skiing, fishing,
    and biking.

Imma New Hampshire
    with this say,
"Come and visit my state
    on your next holiday."

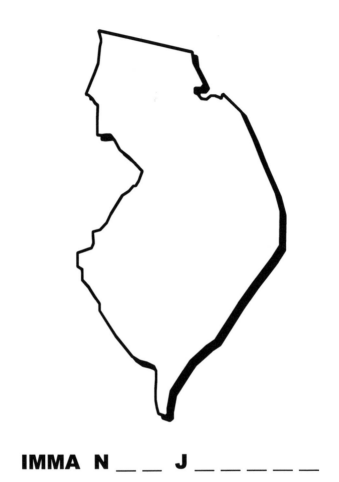

IMMA N _ _ J _ _ _ _ _ _

Imma New Jersey

Imma New Jersey
    or eastern state;
I have a 1787
    birthdate.

I have a profile
    of a person in a hat;
you have to use your imagination
    to see that.

I have mountains, highlands,
    and flatlands to view;
I have farmlands, rivers,
    and beaches, too.

I have Jersey City and Newark
    with a city name;
I have Elizabeth and Trenton
    with a New Jersey claim.

I have cities and towns
    that provide things to see and do;
I also produce many products
    for each of you.

I provide beaches
    for summer fun;
I have swimming and water sports
    and lots of sun.

Imma New Jersey
    with this say,
"Come spend your summers
    on my beaches today."

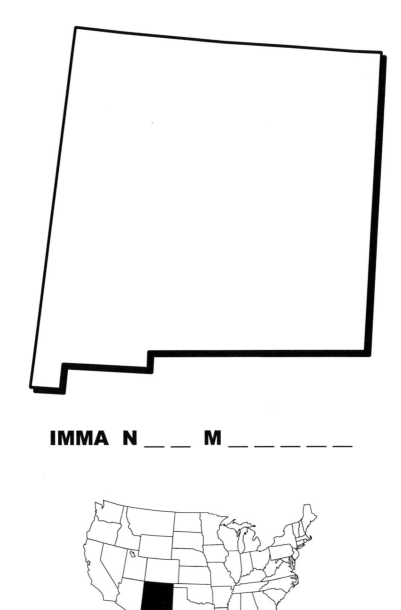

IMMA N _ _ M _ _ _ _ _ _

Imma New Mexico

Imma New Mexico
    or southwestern state;
I have a 1912
    birthdate.

I'm a square state
    with an upside-down building look;
you must use your imagination
    in this Imma book.

I have mountains and plains
    for you to see;
I have sand dunes and mesas
    that characterize me.

I'm a rugged beauty
    for you to view;
I have many sights
    that will intrigue you.

I have "sightful" pueblos
    and historic buildings to see;
I have cliff dwellings
    and caves and caverns that picture me.

I have dams and wells
    and the Rio Grande, too;
I have Santa Fe, the yucca flower,
    and the Santa Fe trail for you.

Imma New Mexico
    with this say,
"You must come and see
    my New Mexico sights today."

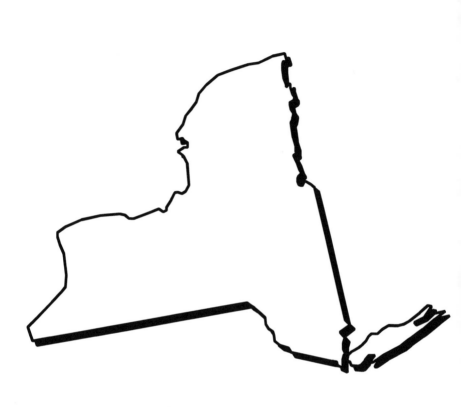

IMMA N _ _ Y _ _ _

Imma New York

Imma New York
 or northeastern state;
I have a 1788
 birthdate.

I'm shaped like a shoe
 or maybe a boot;
you have to use your imagination
 to avoid a dispute.

I have mountains, rivers,
 and lakes to view;
I have waterfalls, streams,
 and lowlands, too.

I have Syracuse and Rochester
 with a city name;
I have Buffalo and New York City
 with a New York claim.

I have tall buildings
 and a deep water port;
I have big bridges
 and many products to report.

I have health resorts
 and musical shows;
I'm the theater capital
 for entertainment pros.

Imma New York
 with this say,
"My New York City
 is called the Big Apple today."

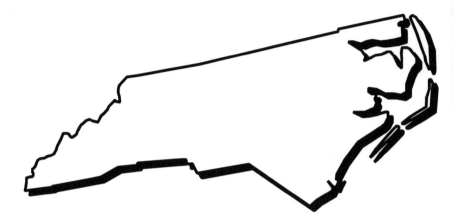

IMMA N _ _ _ _
C _ _ _ _ _ _ _

Imma North Carolina

Imma North Carolina
    or south Atlantic state;
I have a 1789
    birthdate.

I'm shaped like a tool
    or carpenter's plane;
I find a plane
    easy to explain.

I have mountains, hills,
    and a coastal plain;
I have a long and picturesque
    coastal terrain.

I have Durham, Raleigh, and Charlotte
    with a city name;
I have Winston-Salem and Greensboro
    with a North Carolina claim.

I'm both an agricultural
    and industrial state;
I'm a big producer
    with a highly productive rate.

I'm big on food products
    for selling;
I also do furniture
    for home and dwelling.

Imma North Carolina
    with this say,
"You ought to see my furniture
    when it's on display."

IMMA N _ _ _ _
D _ _ _ _ _

Imma North Dakota

Imma North Dakota
    or northwestern state;
I have an 1889
    birthdate.

I have mountains and plains
    for you to see;
I have rivers and lakes
    that picture me.

I'm square in shape
    and of good size;
I'm considered by many
    a farmer's prize.

I'm big in wheat
    and that's what I grow;
I'm a wheat-growing state,
    don't you know.

I have cities and towns
    that support what I do;
I find them helpful
    in supplying wheat to you.

I ship my bushels
    every day;
I ship my wheat
    every which way.

Imma North Dakota
    with this greet,
"I'm also known
    for the sugar beet."

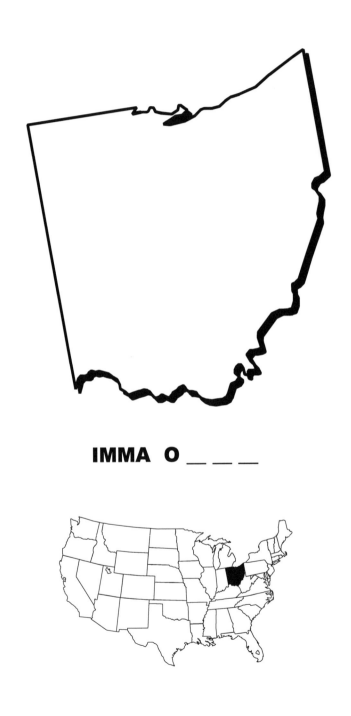

IMMA O _ _ _

Imma Ohio

Imma Ohio
    or north central state;
I have an 1803
    birthdate.

I'm shaped like a spotlight
    if your imagination works well,
but you might have trouble
    with "show and tell."

I have hills and valleys
    for you to see;
I have lakes and rivers
    that picture me.

I have Cleveland and Columbus
    with a city name;
I have Cincinnati and Akron
    with an Ohio claim.

I have many communities
    with nice areas to see;
I have neat neighborhoods
    for my family and me.

I have good schools
    and churches, too;
I have shopping malls
    and services for you.

Imma Ohio
    with this oration,
"I would live in Ohio
    without hesitation."

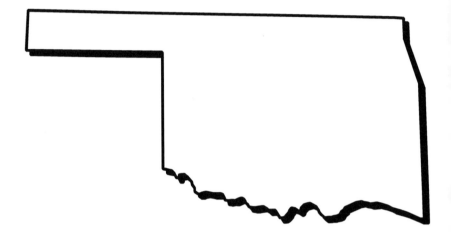

IMMA O _ __ __ __ __ __ __

Imma Oklahoma

Imma Oklahoma
  or southwestern state;
I have a 1907
  birthdate.

I'm shaped like a cannon,
  a western one;
I think it allows your imagination
  to have some fun.

I have mountains and hills
  for you to see;
I have rivers and plains
  that portray me.

I'm a cowboy state
  with ranches and cattle, too;
I have a cowboy culture
  that will intrigue you.

I have Tulsa, Norman, and Lawton
  with a city name;
I have Oklahoma City and Broken Arrow
  with an Oklahoma claim.

I have many Native Americans
  that live with me;
I'm proud to have them
  on my family tree.

Imma Oklahoma
  with this say,
"If you want to see a cowboy culture,
  come down Oklahoma way."

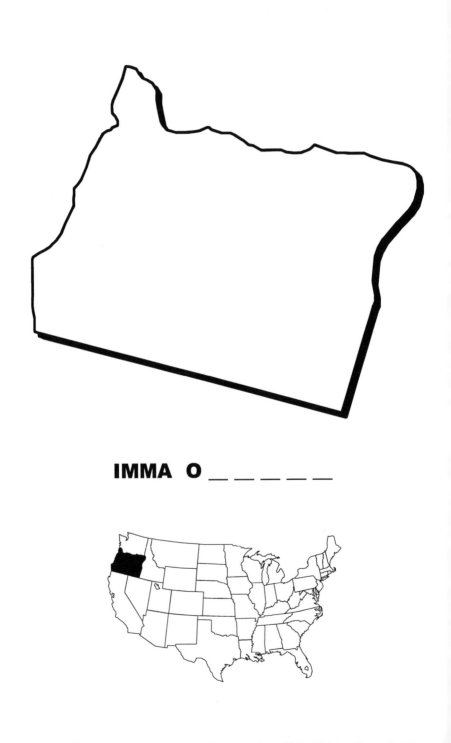

IMMA O _ _ _ _ _ _

Imma Oregon

Imma Oregon
> or northwestern state;
I have an 1859
> birthdate.

I'm square in shape
> and nice in size;
I look like a sled
> imagination-wise.

I have nice forests to view
> and nice rivers to see;
I have mountains and peaks
> that nicely characterize me.

I have Portland and Salem
> with a nice city claim;
I have Eugene and Medford
> with a nice city name.

I have nice buildings and shops
> in each Oregon city;
I have nice flowers and shrubbery
> that make me pretty.

I have nice homes
> and residential sections;
I have nice malls
> in many locations.

Imma Oregon
> with this advice,
"I think you will find Oregon
> to be very nice."

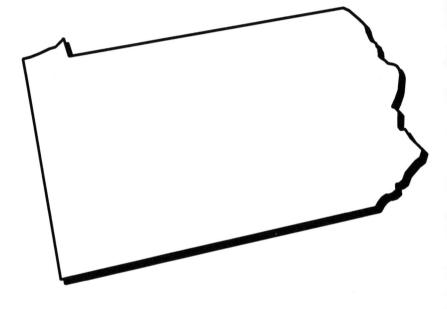

IMMA P _ _ _ _ _ _ _ _ _ _ _ _

Imma Pennsylvania

Imma Pennsylvania
>or middle Atlantic state;
I have a 1787
>birthdate.

I'm a square-shaped state
>with mountains to see;
I have rivers and rolling land
>covering me.

I have cities and towns
>with a historical claim;
I have many places
>with historical fame.

I provided a hall
>to house Congress;
this was in Philadelphia
>and had a Pennsylvania address.

I signed the Declaration of Independence
>in my hall;
this caused the Liberty Bell
>to ring its all.

I drafted the Constitution
>in Philadelphia, too;
I had it written in Pennsylvania
>for you.

Imma Pennsylvania
>with this say,
"Philadelphia was once
>the capital of the U.S.A."

IMMA R _ _ _ _   I _ _ _ _ _ _

Imma Rhode Island

Imma Rhode Island
     or northeastern state;
I have a 1790
     birthdate.

I'm square in shape
     and small in size;
I look like a pitcher
     imagination-wise.

I have a rough and hilly surface
     with a long seacoast;
I have piers and ports
     that are the most.

I have cities and towns
     that enhance all this;
I have a quaintness about me
     that you wouldn't want to miss.

I have lobsters, oysters,
     and clams in my waterways;
I provide fishermen
     with big fishing days.

I'm popular in water sports
     and summer fun;
I offer water-skiing and boating
     with lots of sun.

Imma Rhode Island
     with a word to the wise,
"Don't judge a state
     by its size."

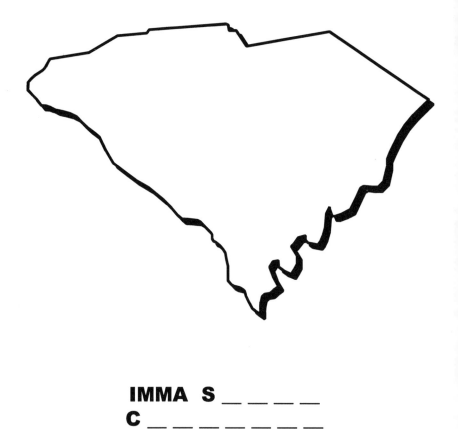

IMMA S _ _ _ _ _
C _ _ _ _ _ _ _ _

Imma South Carolina

Imma South Carolina
        or south Atlantic state;
I have a 1788
        birthdate.

I'm shaped like an animal
        with a head view;
I think you'll need your imagination
        if you want to see, too.

I have lowlands and hills
        and forests to see;
I have mountains, rivers, and a coastal area
        that characterize me.

I have Charleston and Columbia
        with a city name;
I have Greenville and Myrtle Beach
        with a South Carolina claim.

I have communities
        with the old and new;
I have the restored and modern
        just for you.

I have farming and industry
        in my state;
I'm a big producer
        with a high productivity rate.

Imma South Carolina
        with this from my mouth,
"I'm the smallest state
        in the deep South."

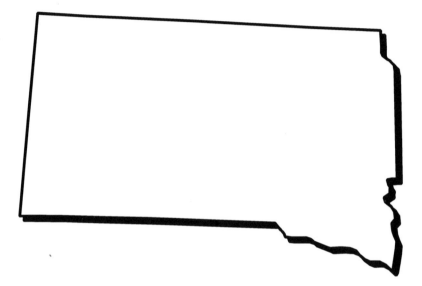

IMMA S _ _ _ _ _   D _ _ _ _ _ _

Imma South Dakota

Imma South Dakota
    or northwestern state;
I have an 1889
    birthdate.

I'm rectangular in shape
    with hills and prairie land;
I have forests and rivers
    with a touch of prairie sand.

I have Sioux Falls and Rapid City
    with a city name;
I have Brookings and Watertown
    with a South Dakota claim.

I have lots to share
    with a cowboy flair;
I have Old West sights
    almost everywhere.

I have the badlands
    for you to see;
I have strange columns and pinnacles
    that characterize me.

I have mines
    that used to have gold;
I find them mined clean
    because they are old.

Imma South Dakota
    with this encore,
"Come see my portrait heads
    on Mount Rushmore."

IMMA T _ _ _ _ _ _ _ _

Imma Tennessee

Imma Tennessee
> or southeastern state;
I have a 1796
> birthdate.

I'm long and narrow
> and have an engine-like shape;
I would call this
> my imagination-scape.

I have big mountains
> and rolling country, too;
I have rivers and lakes
> that are pleasing to view.

I have Memphis, Chattanooga, and Nashville
> with things to see and do;
I provide entertainment,
> historical sites, and activities for you.

I'm big in music
> and do well with the blues;
I have singing
> that musically will amuse.

I have a state name
> that's designed for a spelling bee;
I have a Ten, a Nes,
> and a See in me.

Imma Tennessee
> with this spelling plea,
"Try and spell
> my T__ n n __ s s __ __."

85

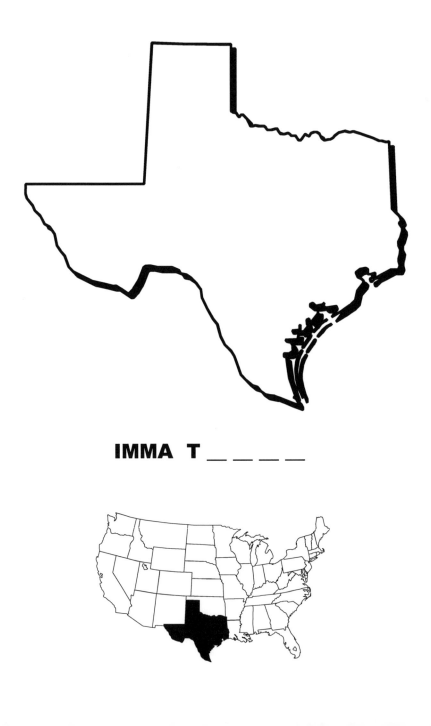

IMMA T _ _ _ _

Imma Texas

Imma Texas
    or southwestern state;
I have an 1845
    birthdate.

I'm a big state
    with a large landscape;
I resemble a steamboat
    on the imagination-scape.

I'm a state
    with a cowboy background;
I wear 10-gallon hats
    and cowboy boots to get around.

I live on ranches
    and raise cattle, too;
I do things
    that you expect cowboys to do.

I have Native Americans
    who live with me;
I'm proud to have them
    on my Texas tree.

I have Dallas, Houston, and San Antonio
    with a cowboy this and that;
they sell spurs, saddles, boots,
    and the 10-gallon hat.

Imma Texas
    with this to declare,
"I'm a state
    with a cowboy flair."

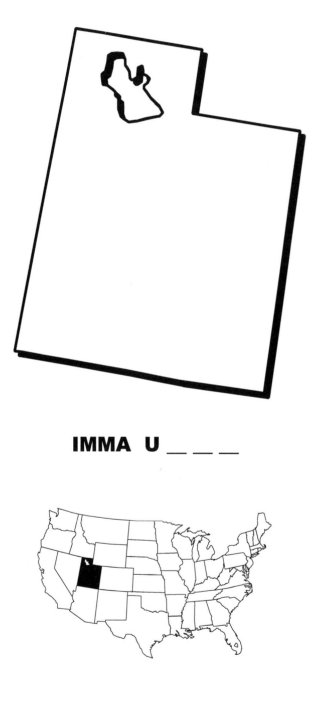

IMMA U _ _ _

Imma Utah

Imma Utah
    or western state;
I have an 1896
    birthdate.

I'm shaped like a building
    with a chimney on top;
I could be a store
    or some kind of a shop.

I have mountains and valleys
    for you to see;
I have rivers, lakes, and deserts
    that characterize me.

I have the largest salt lake
    in North America today;
I can jump in the lake
    and float far away.

I live in a state
    with wonderful cities to see;
I have Salt Lake City, Ogden,
    and Provo that portray me.

I've been helped a lot
    by the Mormon clan;
I've been influenced
    by their special plan.

Imma Utah
    with this say,
"Come and see
    my salt lake today."

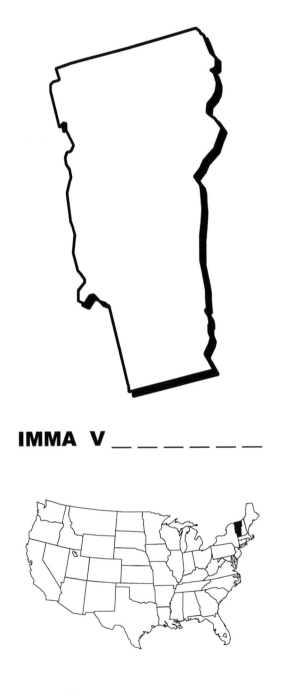

IMMA V _ _ _ _ _ _ _

Imma Vermont

Imma Vermont
   or northeastern state;
I have a 1791
   birthdate.

I'm shaped like a holster
   when you look at me;
I'm long and narrow
   and holster-like to see.

I've got mountains and forests
   with lots of trees;
I've got hills and valleys
   that are sure to please.

I've got cities and towns
   in which to live;
I have farming communities
   that are very active.

I like to farm
   and work the soil;
I find farming
   worth the toil.

I love winter sports
   and what they provide;
I like sledding and skiing
   with the long mountain glide.

Imma Vermont
   with this say,
"Come ski my mountains
   and play."

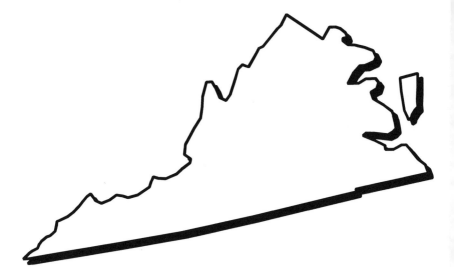

IMMA V _ _ _ _ _ _ _

Imma Virginia

Imma Virginia
     or eastern state;
I have a 1788
     birthdate.

I'm shaped like a plane
     as you can see;
it doesn't take much
     to see a plane in me.

I have Newport News and Norfolk
     with a city name;
I have Richmond and Virginia Beach
     with a Virginia claim.

I've many places
     with old mansions and domes;
I have historical sites
     and Colonial homes.

I have a large naval installation
     and military bases;
I have old battlefields
     and eight presidential birthplaces.

I've restored communities
     and museums to view;
I'm a state
     with the old and new.

Imma Virginia
     with this say,
"You will have much to see,
     when you come my way."

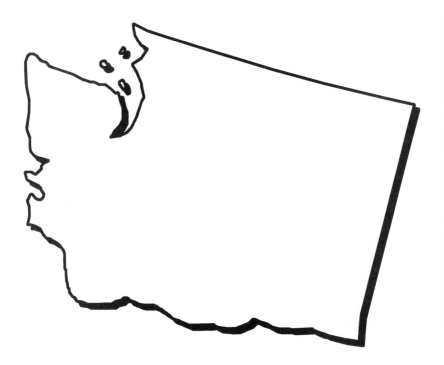

IMMA W _ _ _ _ _ _ _ _ _

Imma Washington

Imma Washington
    or northwestern state;
I have an 1889
    birthdate.

I look like a bird
    watching over my state;
I guess that you will have
    to "imaginate."

I have mountains and valleys
    for you to see;
I have waterfalls and forests
    that picture me.

I have Seattle and Spokane
    with a city claim;
I have Tacoma and Olympia
    with a city name.

I'm a state
    with a productive way;
I have both
    an agricultural and industrial say.

I provide lumber
    and fish for you;
I'm big on apples
    that I produce, too.

Imma Washington
    with this say,
"I contribute a lot
    to my U.S.A."

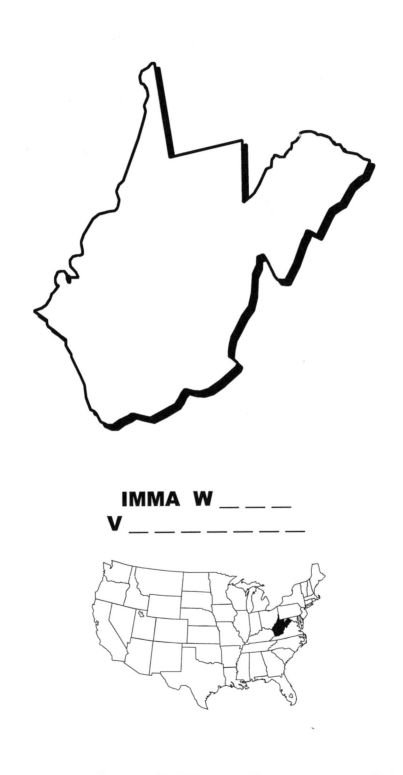

IMMA W _ _ _
V _ _ _ _ _ _ _ _

Imma West Virginia

Imma West Virginia
>or east central state;
I have an 1863
>birthdate.

I'm shaped
>like the top of a frog;
I guess you'll need your imagination
>for this dialogue.

I have hills and mountains
>all around;
I have rivers and streams
>that abound.

I have Wheeling and Charleston
>with a city name;
I have Morgantown and Huntington
>with a West Virginia claim.

I'm an agricultural
>and industrial West Virginia;
I find doing both
>to be a good idea.

I provide city living
>and country life, too;
I find each provides
>a nice life for you.

Imma West Virginia
>with this say,
"I provide a nice place
>to live today."

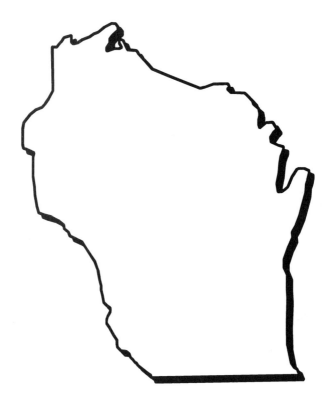

IMMA W _ _ _ _ _ _ _ _ _

Imma Wisconsin

Imma Wisconsin
    or north central state;
I have an 1848
    birthdate.

I'm shaped like an ape
    with its mouth open wide;
I think it looks right
    if you look from the side.

I have flatlands
    with good soil for my ground;
I have many lakes
    that float all around.

I have Green Bay and Milwaukee
    with a city name;
I have Kenosha, Madison, and Racine
    with a Wisconsin claim.

I'm very big
    in milk and cheese;
I also make butter
    that's sure to please.

I find dairy products
    are healthy for you;
I'm now working
    to make them fat-free, too.

Imma Wisconsin
    with this tease,
"You haven't lived
    until you've eaten my cheese."

IMMA W _ _ _ _ _ _

Imma Wyoming

Imma Wyoming
    or western state;
I have an 1890
    birthdate.

I'm rectangular in shape
    and large in size;
I'm a state
    with much to visualize.

I have mountains and lakes
    and plains, too;
I have Yellowstone National Park
    with much to view.

I have lakes of soda
    and hot springs;
I have geysers
    and picturesque mountain openings.

I have deep canyons
    and cataracts;
I have cascades and monuments
    and ancient artifacts.

I have rock formations
    that are awesome to see;
I have beautiful landscapes
    that portray me.

Imma Wyoming
    with this decree,
"Take some time
    and visit me."

Imma's Favorite List

Imma's favorite list
     is made especially for you;
it offers the Imma user
     a special job to do.

It asks you to list
     your favorite poem;
Imma doesn't care
     where you roam.

It asks for a list
     that Imma can see;
it asks for a list
     of 1, 2, or 3.

Now here is the list
     for you to fill in;
here is the list,
     so you can begin.

1. _____

2. _____

3. _____

Imma says thanks
     for your special assist;
you are now a maker
     of Imma's favorite list.

In Conclusion

I hope you've enjoyed
    my Imma book;
it's made for you
    to read and look.

I wanted you to learn
    what states do;
I wanted you to know
    how they relate to you.

A state is a place
    that's here to stay;
a state can touch
    your every day.

A state affects
    every childhood;
a state can touch
    every neighborhood.

So know your states
    and the things they do;
it's important to find out
    how states affect you.

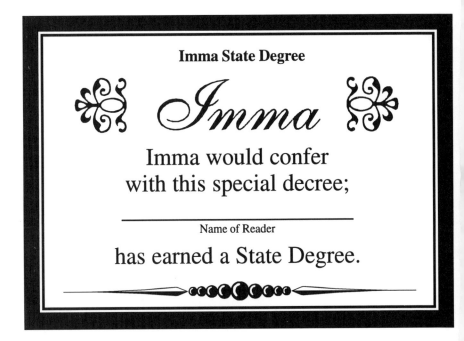

Imma State Degree

Imma

Imma would confer
with this special decree;

_____
Name of Reader

has earned a State Degree.

Imma State Degree

Imma State Degree
    is made especially for you;
it helps to acknowledge
    your state review.

I wanted to state
    that you know state names;
I wanted to state
    that you know state claims.

I wanted to state
    that you have stated well;
I wanted to state
    that you can state spell.

I feel a State Degree
    states a lot;
it kind of states
    what you have state got.

Imma State Degree
    with this final state say,
"I congratulate you
    on your state survey."

The Imma Match Game

Here are some matches
    that Imma made for you;
please match Imma 1
    with Imma 2.

Imma 1

1. Bought from Russia
2. Hot Springs
3. Movies are made
4. Promotes skiing
5. Houses the government
6. Grows oranges
7. Produces pecans
8. An island state
9. Known for potatoes
10. Speedway
11. Horse racing
12. Mardi Gras
13. Crabs
14. An upper and lower peninsula
15. The Old West
16. Entertainment center
17. The theater capital
18. A cowboy culture
19. Historical fame
20. Smallest state in the deep South
21. Mount Rushmore
22. The great salt lake
23. Eight presidents
24. Milk and cheese
25. Yellowstone National Park

Imma 2

____ Wyoming
____ Wisconsin
____ Virginia
____ Utah
____ South Dakota
____ South Carolina
____ Pennsylvania
____ Oklahoma
____ New York
____ Nevada
____ Montana
____ Michigan
____ Maryland
____ Louisiana
____ Kentucky
____ Indiana
____ Idaho
____ Hawaii
____ Georgia
____ Florida
____ District of Columbia
____ Colorado
____ California
____ Arkansas
____ Alaska

Now it's time
    for correcting fun;
so start with 25
    and count back to 1.

A Word About the Author

JERRY T.
by
DONNA T.

    Dr. Tobias was a professor of Education and Human Services at the University of Detroit Mercy. He currently is a practicing counselor in the community. He has a doctorate in education and has trained counselors and counseled for the past 25 years. Jerry loves his work and thinks that his teaching experience and counseling practice blend well together.

    He enjoys writing for young people and has written several youth-oriented books and articles. He writes every day and aims his verse at enriching growth and development. Jerry hopes that his readers will learn from his efforts.

    Jerry has raised six children and believes that his "Imma" books are his seventh child. He researches all the material and then puts it into meaningful rhyme.

    He loves his Imma books and hopes to continue the series in the years to come.

Other Imma Books
By
Jerry Tobias

Imma Fruit
Imma Tool
Imma Vegetable
Imma Community Helper
Imma Doctor's Office
Imma Color
Imma Musical Instrument
Imma Insect
Imma Animal
Imma Bird
Imma Flower
Imma Hospital
Imma Drug
Imma Fish
Imma Sportsperson
Imma Culture

Coming Soon . . .

Imma Child Protector

Ask for an Imma book
at your local bookstore
or write:

Jerry Tobias
Teddy Bear Press
P.O. Box 503
Bloomfield Hills,
Michigan 48303
(248) 851-8607
www.techsource.com/imma